THE ADVENTURES OF AMAZING MAZERS

HIDDEN PICTURES AND MAZE GAMES

By

Christine San José, Ph.D., and Jody Taylor

Boyds Mills Press

Illustrated by Charles Jordan

ADVENTURES ON THE
ZAMTONGO RIVER

When Professor Percy Pearce did not appear for tea on Tuesday, the Amazing Mazers knew something was wrong. Upon investigation, they learned that the Professor had last been seen leaving for a secret expedition down the treacherous Zamtongo River.

Max, Millie, and Master immediately set out to find their missing friend. Entering the mouth of the Zamtongo, they discovered Professor Pearce's toothbrush. Had the Professor left a trail to his whereabouts? Starting with the **toothbrush,** can you help the Mazers find the **teacup, ballpoint pen, spoon, wristwatch, compass, magnifying glass, book, bowl,** and the **pencil** that will show them the path to their friend?

Answers on page 30.

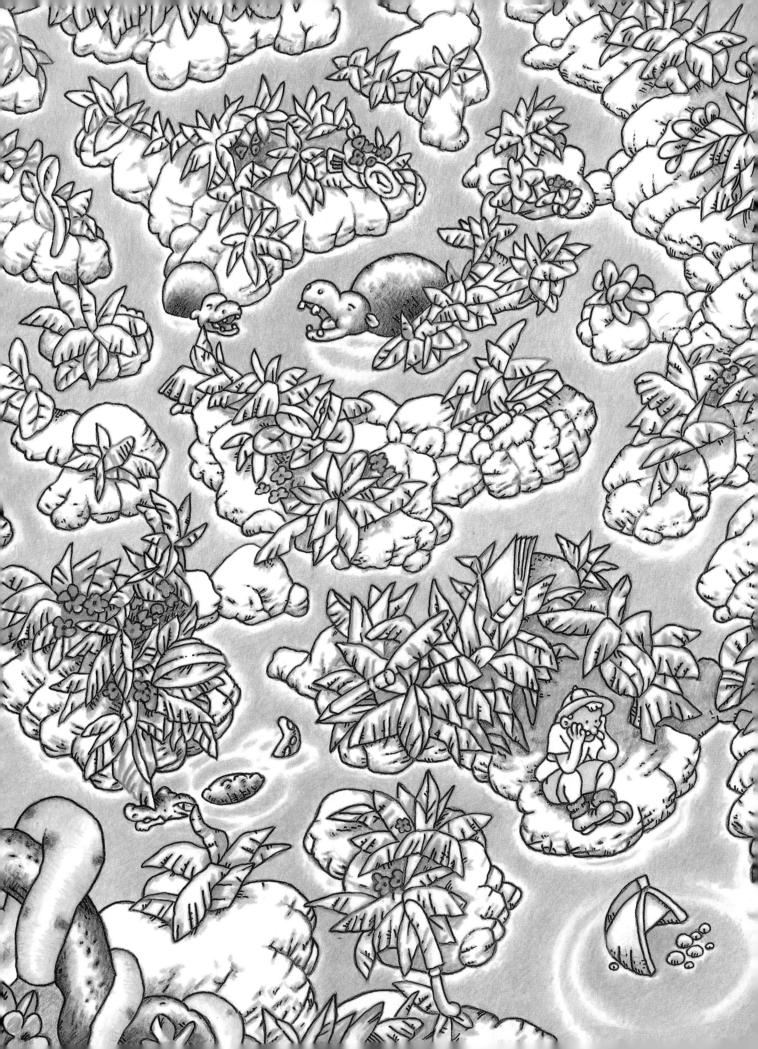

ADVENTURES IN
OUTER SPACE

The Mazers' spacecraft was blasted by a meteor shower. The shower ripped off the cargo doors. The ship's supplies were pulled out into space. Now the space travelers need to launch a recovery mission.

Millie and Max have assigned Master to recover the supplies and meet them at Space Station One. Master's mini-ship is very low on fuel.

Help him find the shortest path between the meteors, picking up as many supplies as he can on his way to the space station.

The cargo log shows that the following 20 items are missing: a **fruit bowl, horseshoe, violin, hairbrush, hammer, tennis racket, alarm clock, bell, scissors, shoe, binoculars, space bike, mug, wishbone, bugle, camera, teapot, magnifying glass, whistle,** and **magic lamp.** Which ones of these can Master recover on his way? Which ones will he have to leave in orbit forever?

Answers on page 30.

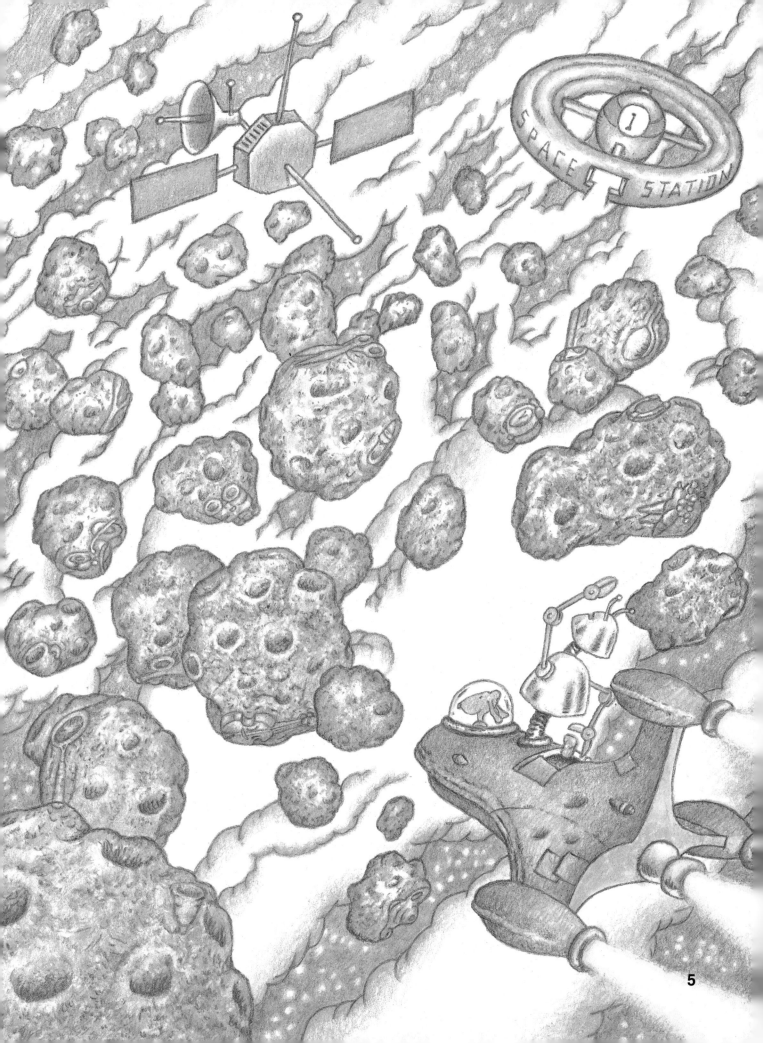

5

Look what Master found on the beach. Can you help Max and Millie find the treasure?

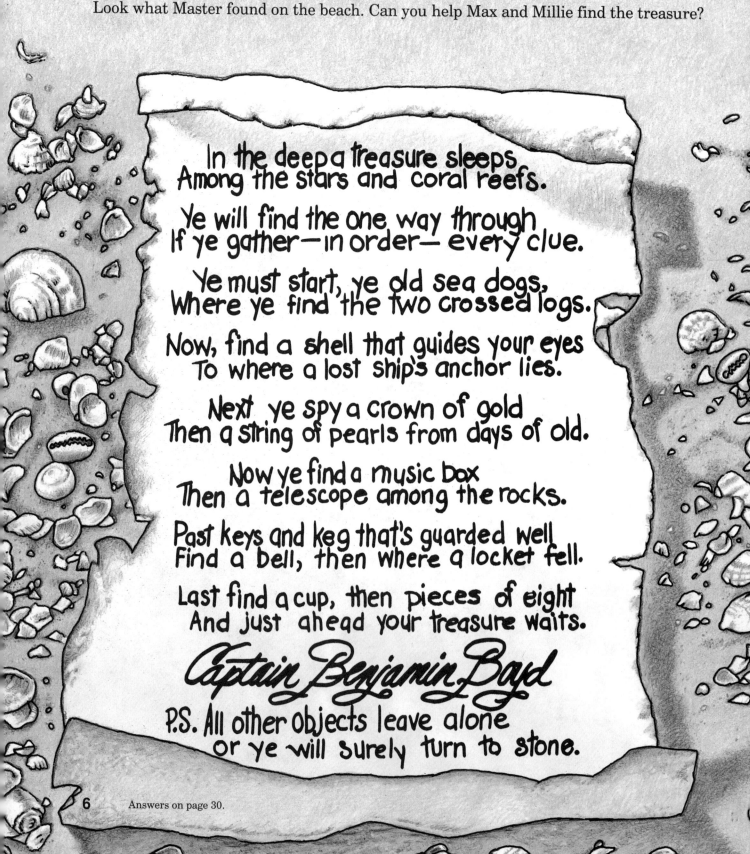

In the deep a treasure sleeps,
Among the stars and coral reefs.

Ye will find the one way through
If ye gather—in order—every clue.

Ye must start, ye old sea dogs,
Where ye find the two crossed logs.

Now, find a shell that guides your eyes
To where a lost ship's anchor lies.

Next ye spy a crown of gold
Then a string of pearls from days of old.

Now ye find a music box
Then a telescope among the rocks.

Past keys and keg that's guarded well
Find a bell, then where a locket fell.

Last find a cup, then pieces of eight
And just ahead your treasure waits.

Captain Benjamin Boyd

P.S. All other objects leave alone
or ye will surely turn to stone.

ADVENTURES IN
The Backyard

The Amazing Mazers were needed for another top secret mission. But where was their cunning canine companion, Master? This super sniffer was nowhere to be found.

"Sometimes that dog takes secrecy too far," muttered Millie. "He's left a trail of hidden treats and objects behind. Let's remember what we've seen him with this week and track him down. First there was that **old peanut butter jar,** then he had a **dried-up paintbrush,** then Dad's **old shoe,** and then the **wishbone** from Sunday dinner, his favorite **crayon,** a **cupcake,** the **backdoor key,** a **cup and saucer, decoder ring,** a **golf club,** a **feather,** and just today he had that **plastic ice-cream cone.**"

Can you help the Mazers pick up their pup and hurry off to save the day?

Answers on page 30.

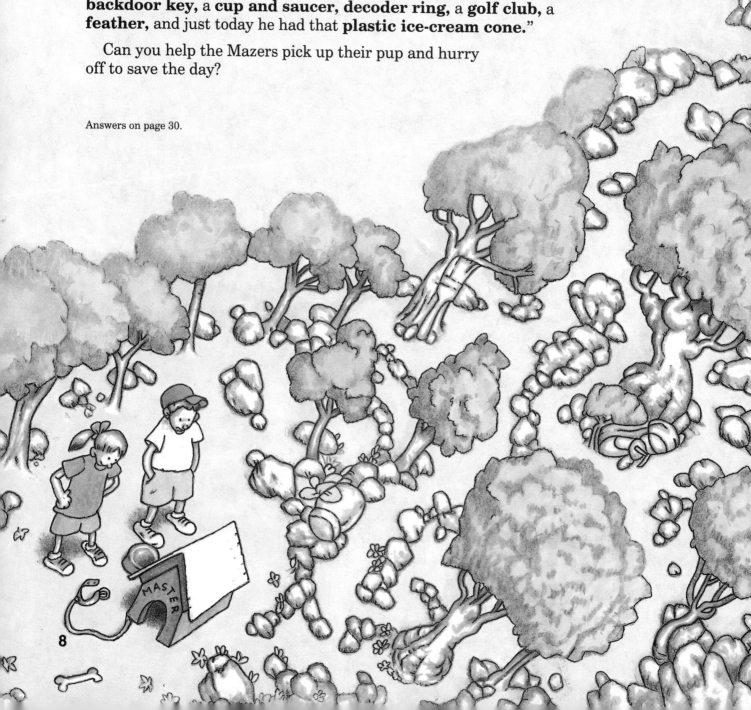

8

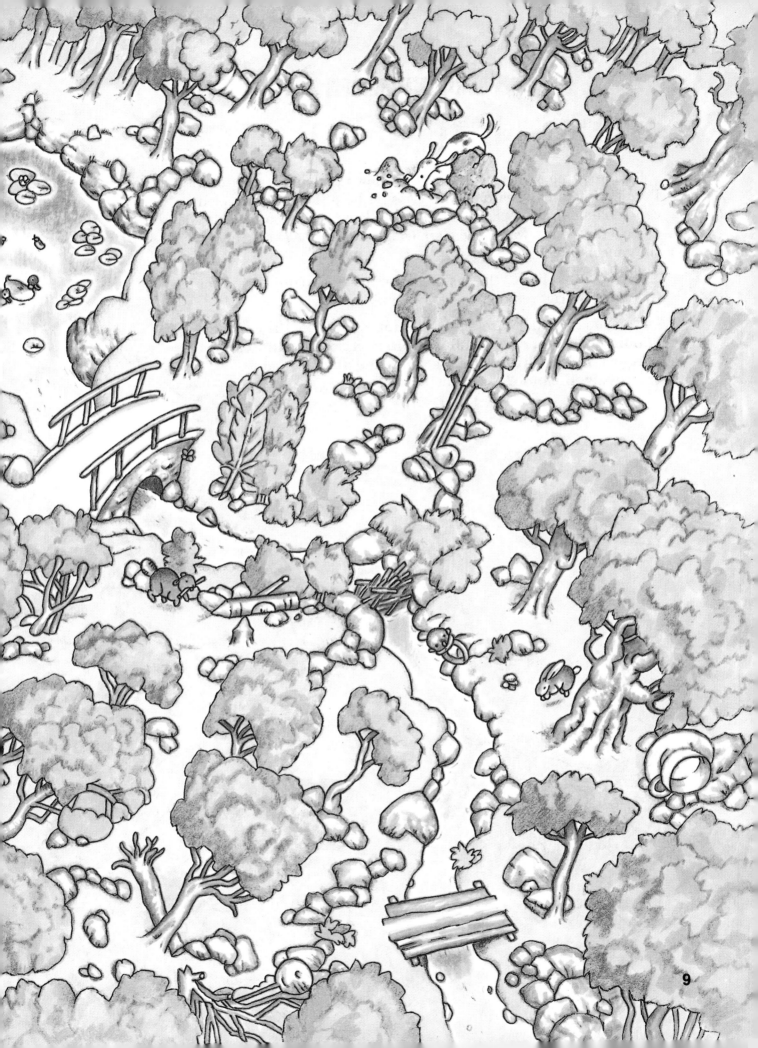

ADVENTURES ON
THE RIO PERDIDO

The Amazing Mazers were canoeing down the white water of the Rio Perdido when they heard distant cries for help. The Mazers spied a canteen among the rocks and knew exactly what had happened. The treacherous white water had claimed another canoe and stranded the canoeists along the rocky shores.

"Max," said Millie, "the rushing river has left a trail of gear for us to follow. We can rescue those travelers."

Can you help the Mazers find the trail marked by the **canteen, spoon, compass, one paddle, apple core, mug, sandwich, camera, flashlight, backpack, another paddle,** and the **capsized canoe?**

Answers on page 30.

10

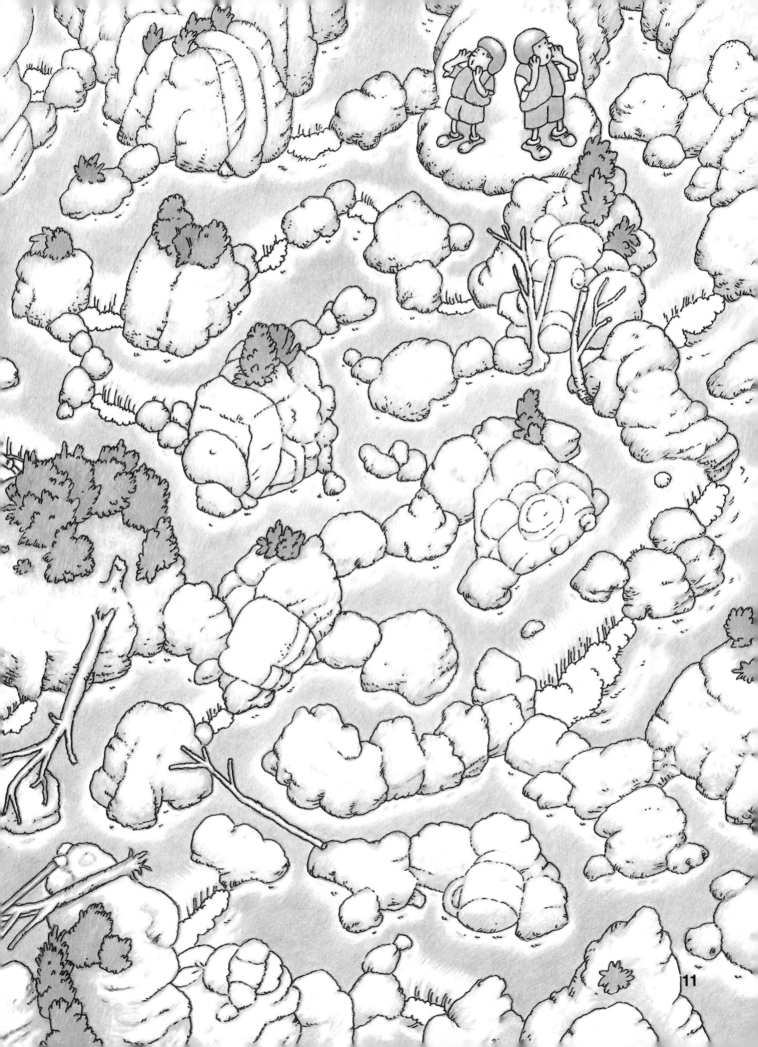

ADVENTURES AT
The Tour deFranz

Shortly after the great bike race began, the Mazers received a desperate message from their teammate, Pierre. "Help! My super-speed, custom-built, cross-country titanium bicycle has collapsed into a unicycle. There will be no hope of our winning the Grand Championship unless we rebuild my magnificent machine at once. You must recover my **screwdriver, pocketknife, wing nut, air pump, bolt, screw, wrench, water bottle, pliers, toolbox, roll of tape, hammer,** and **oilcan** that fell off along the bike-rally route."

Help the Mazers assist their pedaling pal, Pierre, out of peril and pursue the prize.

Answers on page 30.

12

ADVENTURES AT
THE DINO DIG

The famous dinosaur experts, Dr. Evan and Dr. Hadden, invited the Mazers to their dinosaur dig. They searched for the nest of the *Triceratops*.

"We know the trail is marked by 12 hidden dinosaur bones," revealed the paleontologists. "Each bone we find will lead us closer to the nest."

Can you help these dinosaur detectives find the **12 huge bones** marking the trail to the nest and an unbelievable discovery?

Answers on page 31.

ADVENTURES UNDER
THE BIG TOP

The circus was in town for only a few hours when the Amazing Mazers were summoned to the big top. Colonel Phineas T. Bigelow, the world's greatest ringmaster, was alarmed. He told the Mazers that the star attraction of the circus, Wally, the Wild White Monkey, had disappeared.

"And he stole my bag of peanuts, too," grumbled the Colonel.

"Aha," said the Mazers. "Then we'll soon be on his trail."

Can you help the Amazing Mazers find the **12 peanut shells** that will lead them to the missing monkey?

Answers on page 31.

ADVENTURES IN
The Marble Canyon

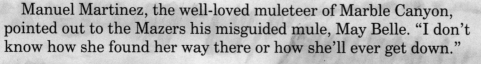

Manuel Martinez, the well-loved muleteer of Marble Canyon, pointed out to the Mazers his misguided mule, May Belle. "I don't know how she found her way there or how she'll ever get down."

"What a mysterious mishap," murmured the Mazers. "But if she found her way there, so can we. This canyon is littered with clues that she dropped from her pack. Let's start with the **knife** and wind our way through the canyon gathering up the **magnifying glass, wristwatch, ball-point pen, purse, spoon, book, canteen, pencil, teacup, hairbrush,** and then that muddled mule."

Can you help the Mazers and Manuel find the clues, the path, and the unfortunate May Belle?

Answers on page 31.

ADVENTURES IN
THE TUNDRA

The Amazing Mazers were practicing for the Tundra Dog Sled Race when they heard the sputtering engine of Major Merryweather's helicopter. Falling from the sky came a **screw, spring, light bulb, pliers, bolt, hammer, screwdriver, wrench, flashlight, saw, spark plug, key,** and an **oilcan**. Then Major Merryweather and her copter suddenly dropped from sight.

Immediately the Mazers backtracked and mushed right to find the screw, then followed the trail of the rest of the fallen chopper cargo. The Major had to be rescued before night and the temperature fell.

Can you help the Mushing Mazers rush to the aid of Major Merryweather?

Answers on page 31.

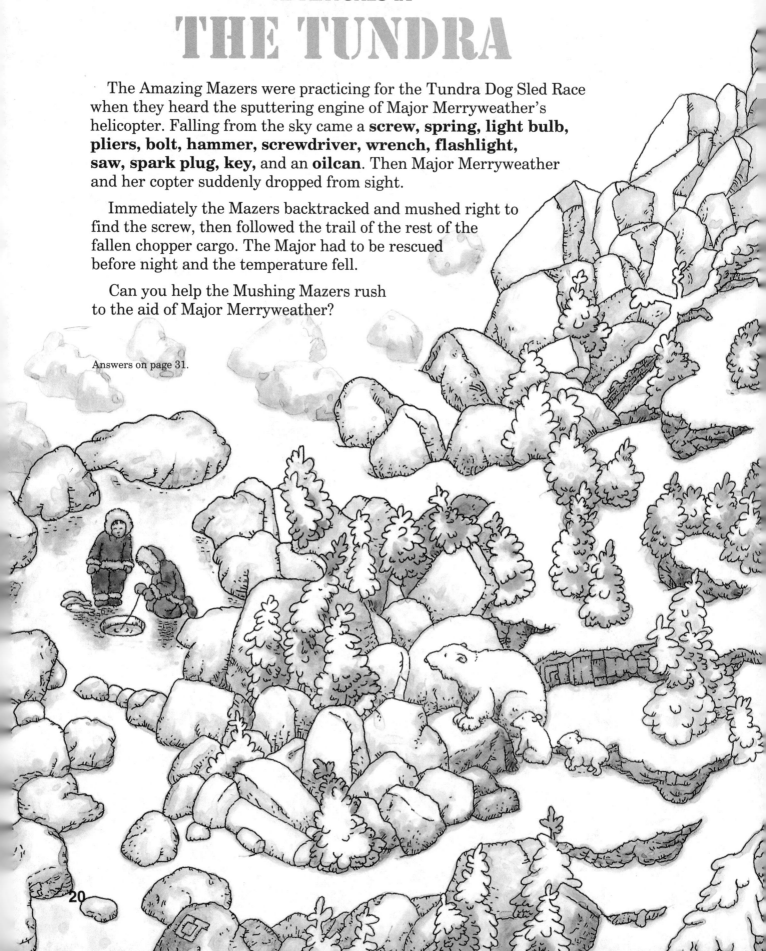

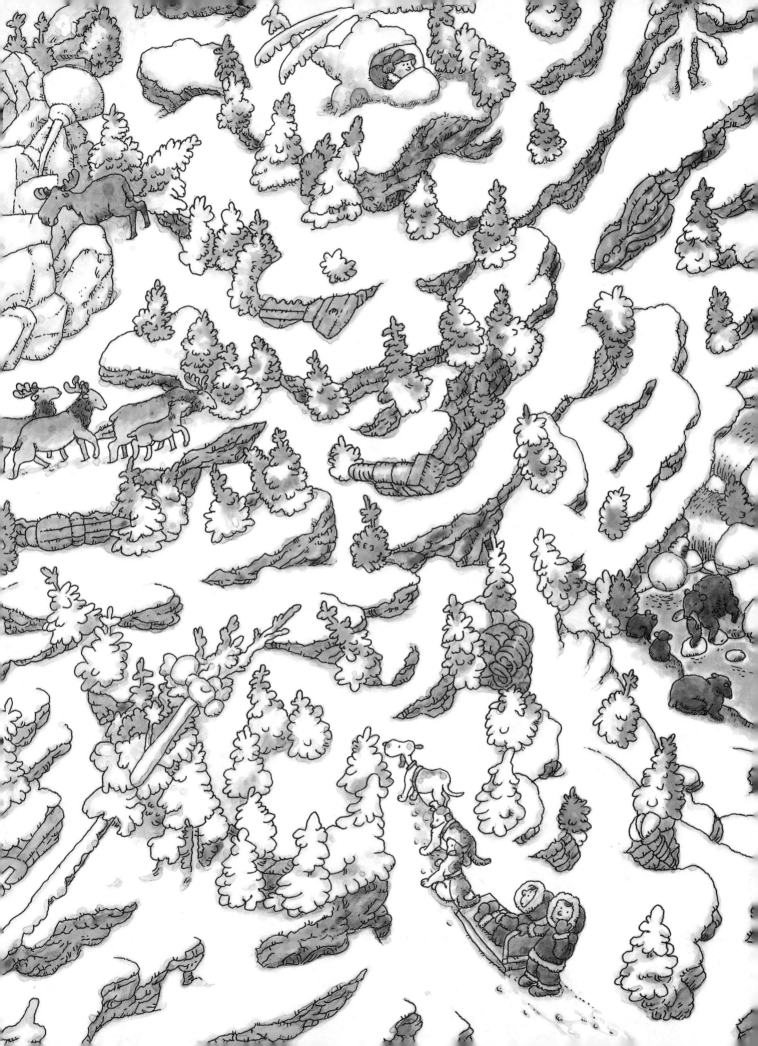

ADVENTURES AT
The Ancient Ruins

Professor Santiago summoned Max and Millie to help him find the treasure of the double-headed serpent. When they arrived, he revealed to them his latest discovery, a carved-stone chart. It was the missing clue that explained the way to the prize. Professor Santiago chanted the directions:

"Ye who seek the serpent, see first the circle chart.
Begin with fish—then, on the path, hidden **fish** is where you start.
Next comes armadillo in the stone chart round.
So travel far along your path to hidden **armadillo**'s ground.
In turn each creature round the stone will lead ye to your prize,
If ye seek out along the path where the hidden likeness lies.
Shun all other creatures that hide and lie in wait.
To reach the serpent treasure, follow only the chart's true eight."

Answers on page 31.

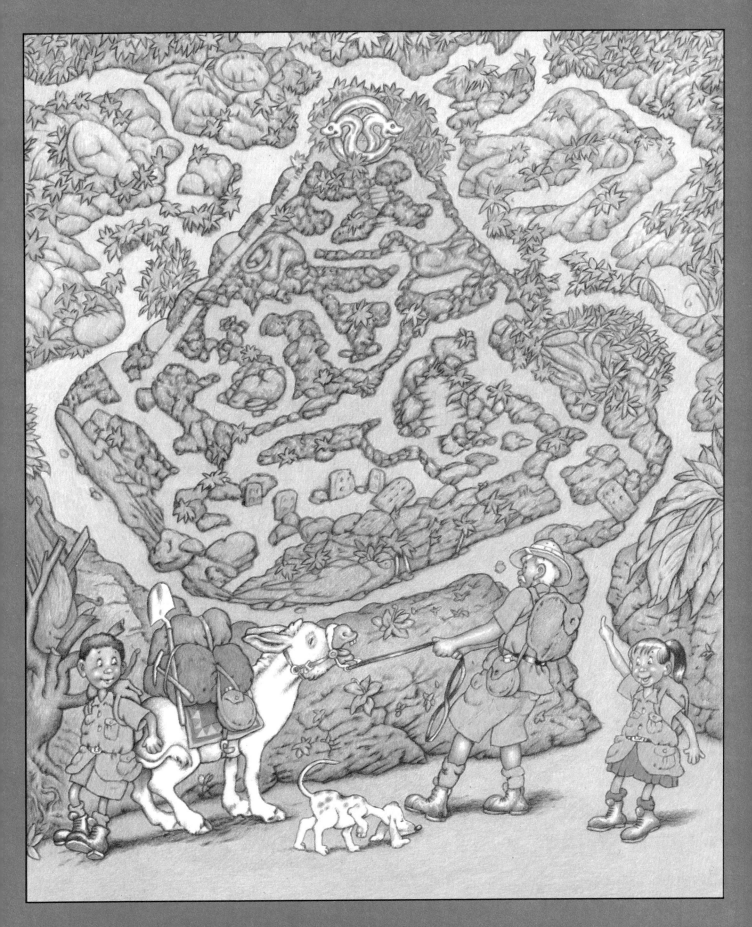

ADVENTURES AT
THE OASIS

Those renowned experts on ancient Egypt, Colonel Pitchett and Professor Gamal, sent an urgent message to the Mazers asking to meet them at the oasis on Tuesday at 7:00 A.M. sharp. When the Mazers arrived, the men explained that a wondrous treasure had been stolen from the museum.

"Our museum had just been given a **bowl, emerald, walking stick, snake bracelet, copper pitcher, diamond, chalice,** King Zoser's **sandal, scarab, ring,** and the famous Queen of Zoser's **scroll,**" said Professor Gamal. "As soon as we had them on display, everything mysteriously vanished. Later that evening I received a strange telephone call saying that the treasure could be found at this oasis."

Can you help the Mazers and the Egyptologists with this historic treasure hunt?

Answers on page 31.

ADVENTURES IN
The Lost Clementine Mine

Uncle Mac Mazer found the largest pocket of gold this side of the Pecos. But he had to stake his claim within 24 hours. But who would guard the gold from claim jumpers and bandits while he was gone?

Uncle Mac sent a message to Max, Millie, and Master for their help. When they arrived, he told them how to locate the shaft containing the gold nuggets. "Ain't gonna say this but once, so listen hard and listen good. This mine is dangerous and ain't to be trusted. I've marked the trail with my own gear. Find my gear and you'll be safe. Stray off the path and you'll be in big trouble."

Help these mini-miners find the trail to the gold by locating all 12 of Uncle Mac's mining tools: a **jar**, **pail**, **ladle**, **hammer**, **canteen**, **ax**, **pick**, **pocket watch**, **mug**, **candle**, **pan**, and a **coffee pot**.

Answers on page 31.

ADVENTURES IN
THE KING'S GARDEN

The Mazers were summoned by the Royal Caterpillar Keeper and the famous Royal Entomologist of the King's Court Garden. They had a dilemma, and time was running out. Twenty rare royal green caterpillars had escaped from the royal greenhouse.

"They must be captured and returned to this royal brown box," said Royal Caterpillar Keeper Countess Caroline.

"These rare royal green caterpillars are in real danger," pointed out the famous Royal Entomologist Eileen. "They could even turn yellow!"

Can you help the Mazers gather up these **20** rare royal green **caterpillars** before darkness falls on the royal garden? You'll have to stretch with that net!

Answers on page 31.

ANSWERS

PAGE 6-7: Adventures in the Deep

PAGE 2-3: Adventures on the Zamtongo River

PAGE 8-9: Adventures in the Backyard

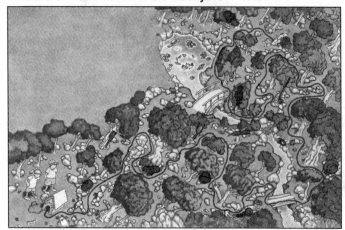

PAGE 4-5: Adventures in Outer Space

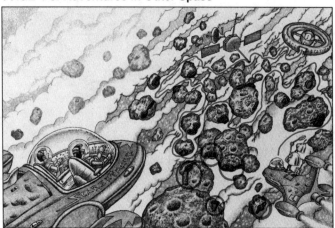

PAGE 10-11: Adventures on the Rio Perdido

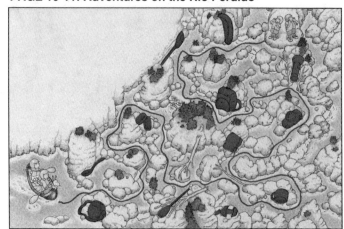

PAGE 4-5: Adventures in Outer Space

Items recovered include:

1. fruit bowl	9. space bike
2. horseshoe	10. mug
3. hairbrush	11. wishbone
4. hammer	12. camera
5. alarm clock	13. teapot
6. scissors	14. magnifying glass
7. shoe	15. whistle
8. binoculars	

Items left to orbit:

1. magic lamp	4. bugle
2. bell	5. violin
3. tennis racket	

PAGE 12-13: Adventures at the Tour deFranz

30

PAGE 14-15: Adventures at the Dino Dig

PAGE 16-17: Adventures under the Big Top

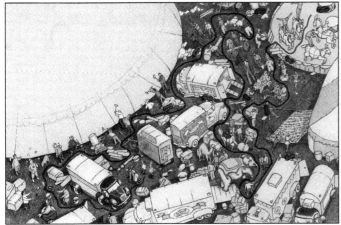

PAGE 18-19: Adventures in the Marble Canyon

PAGE 20-21: Adventures in the Tundra

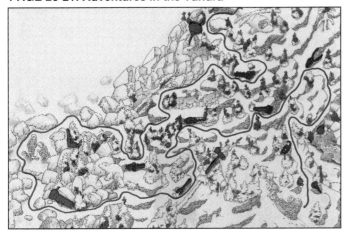

PAGE 22-23: Adventures at the Ancient Ruins

PAGE 24-25: Adventures at the Oasis

PAGE 26-27: Adventures in the Lost Clementine Mine

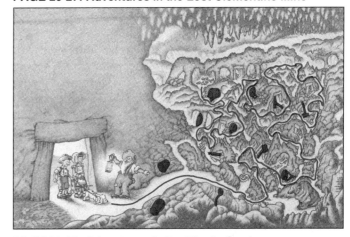

PAGE 28-29: Adventures in the King's Garden

Published by Bell Books
Boyds Mills Press, Inc.
A Highlights Company
815 Church Street
Honesdale, Pennsylvania 18431
Printed in the United States of America

Publisher Cataloging-in-Publication Data
San José, Christine.
The adventures of the amazing mazers : hidden pictures and maze games /
by Christine San José and Jody Taylor ;
illustrated by Charles Jordan.—1st ed.
[32]p. : col. ill. ; cm.
Summary : To find their way through the mazes, readers are asked to find the hidden
objects within the pictures.
ISBN 1-56397-335-9
1. Picture puzzles—Juvenile literature. [1. Picture puzzles.]
I. Taylor, Jody. II. Jordan, Charles, ill. III. Title.
793.73—dc20   1994
Library of Congress Catalog Card Number 93-72341

First edition, 1994
Book designed by Tim Gillner
The text of this book is set in 12-point New Century Schoolbook.
The illustrations are done in colored pencil.
Distributed by St. Martin's Press

10 9 8 7 6 5 4 3 2